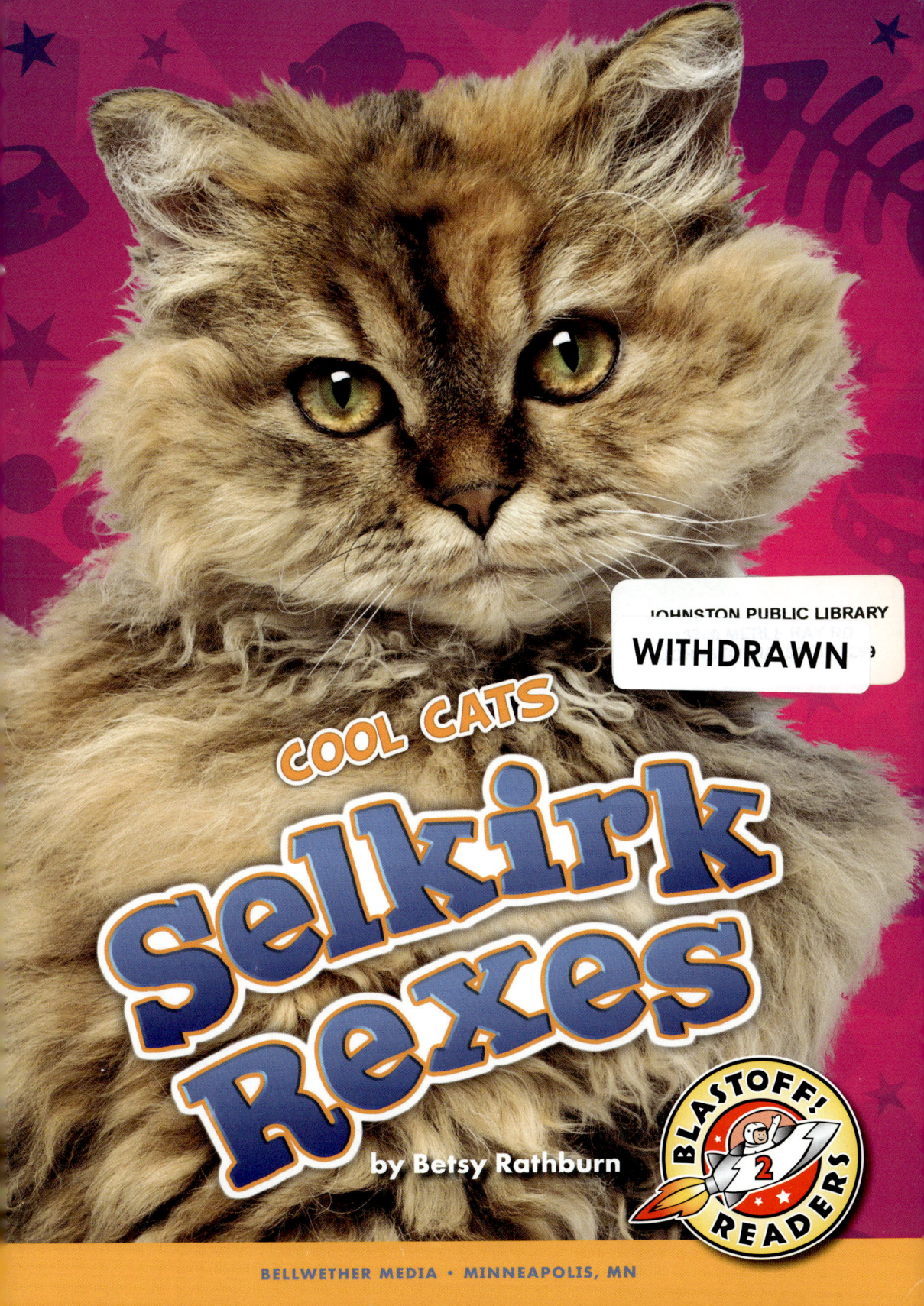

COOL CATS

Selkirk Rexes

by Betsy Rathburn

Note to Librarians, Teachers, and Parents:

Blastoff! Readers are carefully developed by literacy experts and combine standards-based content with developmentally appropriate text.

Level 1 provides the most support through repetition of high-frequency words, light text, predictable sentence patterns, and strong visual support.

Level 2 offers early readers a bit more challenge through varied simple sentences, increased text load, and less repetition of high-frequency words.

Level 3 advances early-fluent readers toward fluency through increased text and concept load, less reliance on visuals, longer sentences, and more literary language.

Level 4 builds reading stamina by providing more text per page, increased use of punctuation, greater variation in sentence patterns, and increasingly challenging vocabulary.

Level 5 encourages children to move from "learning to read" to "reading to learn" by providing even more text, varied writing styles, and less familiar topics.

Whichever book is right for your reader, Blastoff! Readers are the perfect books to build confidence and encourage a love of reading that will last a lifetime!

This edition first published in 2017 by Bellwether Media, Inc.

No part of this publication may be reproduced in whole or in part without written permission of the publisher. For information regarding permission, write to Bellwether Media, Inc., Attention: Permissions Department, 5357 Penn Avenue South, Minneapolis, MN 55419.

Library of Congress Cataloging-in-Publication Data

Names: Rathburn, Betsy, author.
Title: Selkirk Rexes / by Betsy Rathburn.
Other titles: Blastoff! Readers. 2, Cool Cats.
Description: Minneapolis, MN : Bellwether Media, Inc., [2017] | Series: Blastoff! Readers. Cool Cats | Audience: Ages 5-8. | Audience: K to grade 3. | Includes bibliographical references and index.
Identifiers: LCCN 2016032037 (print) | LCCN 2016040362 (ebook) | ISBN 9781626175648 (hardcover : alk. paper) | ISBN 9781681032856 (ebook)
Subjects: LCSH: Rex cat–Juvenile literature. | Cat breeds–Juvenile literature.
Classification: LCC SF449.R4 R38 2017 (print) | LCC SF449.R4 (ebook) | DDC 636.8/22–dc23
LC record available at https://lccn.loc.gov/2016032037

Text copyright © 2017 by Bellwether Media, Inc. BLASTOFF! READERS and associated logos are trademarks and/or registered trademarks of Bellwether Media, Inc. SCHOLASTIC, CHILDREN'S PRESS, and associated logos are trademarks and/or registered trademarks of Scholastic Inc.

Editor: Christina Leaf   Designer: Lois Stanfield

Printed in the United States of America, North Mankato, MN.

Table of Contents

What Are Selkirk Rexes? 4
History of Selkirk Rexes 8
Colorful Curls 12
Silly and Sweet 18
Glossary 22
To Learn More 23
Index 24

What Are Selkirk Rexes?

Selkirk rexes are cats with curly **coats**. Even their whiskers curl!

Some people call them cats in sheep's clothing. Others call them poodle cats.

Selkirk rexes can have short or long hair. Their coats feel **plush**.

They are curliest around their bellies and necks. Long-haired Selkirk rexes have **ruffs**.

ruff

History of Selkirk Rexes

Montana, United States

In 1987, a curly-haired kitten was born in Montana. She was named Miss DePesto.

Jeri Newman **bred** her with a Persian cat. More curly-haired cats were born!

Newman named the new **breed** after her stepfather. It is the only breed named after a person.

"Rex" was added to match other curly-haired cats.

Colorful Curls

Some Selkirk rex kittens have straight hair. They look like ordinary cats.

Curly-haired kittens lose their curls as they grow. But they return when the cats are adults!

These cats come in any color or pattern. They are often red, blue, or brown.

Tabby and **calico** are common patterns.

Selkirk rexes have **stocky** bodies. Their legs are strong. They have big, round eyes and chubby cheeks.

Selkirk Rex Profile

- round eyes
- round head
- stocky body
- curly hair

Weight: 6 to 16 pounds (3 to 7 kilograms)

Life Span: 10 to 15 years

Silly and Sweet

Selkirk rexes are calm and **patient** cats. They do not mind being pet by strangers.

They are silly, too. Games like chasing toys or playing tag excite them.

Selkirk rexes are sweet and **affectionate**.

They curl up with their owners. Selkirk rexes are great cats to cuddle!

Glossary

affectionate—loving

bred—purposely mated two cats to make kittens with certain qualities

breed—a type of cat

calico—a pattern that has patches of white, black, and reddish brown fur

coats—the hair or fur covering some animals

patient—able to stay calm in difficult situations

plush—very thick and soft

ruffs—areas of longer fur around the necks of some animals

stocky—thick in build

tabby—a pattern that has stripes, patches, or swirls of colors

To Learn More

AT THE LIBRARY
Felix, Rebecca. *Persians*. Minneapolis, Minn.: Bellwether Media, 2016.

Leaf, Christina. *Devon Rexes*. Minneapolis, Minn.: Bellwether Media, 2016.

Petrie, Kristin. *Selkirk Rex Cats*. Minneapolis, Minn.: ABDO Publishing Company, 2014.

ON THE WEB
Learning more about Selkirk rexes is as easy as 1, 2, 3.

1. Go to www.factsurfer.com.

2. Enter "Selkirk rexes" into the search box.

3. Click the "Surf" button and you will see a list of related web sites.

With factsurfer.com, finding more information is just a click away.

Index

bellies, 7
bodies, 16, 17
bred, 9
breed, 10
cheeks, 16
coats, 4, 6, 15
color, 14
cuddle, 21
curly, 4, 7, 8, 9, 11, 13, 17
eyes, 16, 17
games, 19
hair, 6, 12, 17
kitten, 8, 12, 13
legs, 16
life span, 17
Miss DePesto, 8
Montana, 8

name, 10, 11
necks, 7
Newman, Jeri, 9, 10
nicknames, 5
owners, 21
patterns, 14, 15
Persian, 9
ruffs, 7
size, 17
tag, 19
toys, 19
whiskers, 4

The images in this book are reproduced through the courtesy of: Eric Isselee, front cover, pp. 15 (upper left), 16-17 (cat), 17, 18; mdmmikle/ Can Stock Photo, p. 4; Tetsu Yamazaki/ Animal-Photography, pp. 4-5 (cat), 7, 15 (lower left); mangpor2004, pp. 4-5 (background); Ron Kimball/ Kimball Stock, pp. 6-7; Juniors Bildarchiv GmbH/ Alamy, pp. 8-9 (kittens), 11, 14-15; zhu difeng, pp. 8-9 (background); Tierfotoagentur/ Alamy, pp. 12-13, 18-19 (kitten); mdmmikle, pp. 13, 15 (upper right); Bigandt_Photography, p. 15 (lower right); Brian S, pp. 16-17 (background); Charts and BG, pp. 18-19 (background); Jagodka, p. 19; fotojagodka, p. 20; Alex Milan Tracy/ Newscom, p. 21.